A Whiff of Pizza

by Frances Ann Ladd

Illustrated by Duendes del Sur

SCHOLASTIC INC.
New York   Toronto   London   Auckland   Sydney
Mexico City   New Delhi   Hong Kong   Buenos Aires

D0888270

It was time for dinner.
Shaggy set the table.
"Where are the plates?"
said Shaggy.
"There they are.
Now, where is Scooby?"

He called for Scooby.
"Scooby,
where are you?"
He whistled three times.
Scooby did not come.
So Shaggy went out
to find him.

Then he sniffed a whiff
of something good.
"Oh, brother!
I know what
that smell is!"
Shaggy said.
"That is the smell
of pizza!"

Scooby was outside, too.
He was hungry.
He whined.
He whimpered.
Then he smelled a whiff
of something good.
He followed his nose.

Shaggy did not
see Scooby.
Scooby did not
see Shaggy.
Wham!
They ran right into
each other!
"Whoops!" said Shaggy.

"There you are, Scooby!
And, like,
what do you know?
I am hungry and thirsty.
And we are at
the pizza place!"
said Shaggy.

"What do you want
to eat, Scooby?"
Scooby wanted whatever
Shaggy wanted.
Shaggy ordered a pizza
with a thin crust.
Together they ate
the whole thing.

Then they got
another pizza
and ate that one, too!